Printed in Great Britain
by Amazon

86469059R00071